WO SMITH

Beijing Breakaway!

written by
anne Sautel

illustrated by
Scott Stewart

Lobster Press™

Published by Lobster Press™
1620 Sherbrooke Street West, Suites C & D
Montréal, Québec   H3H 1C9
Tel. (514) 904-1100 • Fax (514) 904-1101 • www.lobsterpress.com

Publisher: Alison Fripp
Editors: Alison Fripp & Meghan Nolan
Editorial Assistants: Morgan Dambergs & Olga Zoumboulis
Graphic Design & Production: Tammy Desnoyers

We acknowledge the financial support of the Government of Canada
through the Book Publishing Industry Development Program (BPIDP)
for our publishing activities.

The Canada Council   Le Conseil des Arts
for the Arts   du Canada

We acknowledge the support of
the Canada Council for the Arts
for our publishing program.

Library and Archives Canada Cataloguing in Publication

Sautel, Anne, 1934-
        Beijing breakaway! / Anne Sautel ; illustrated by Scott Stewart.

(Wombat Smith ; v. 2)
ISBN-13: 978-1-897073-48-3
ISBN-10: 1-897073-48-8

        1. Marsupials--Juvenile literature. I. Stewart, Scott, 1971-
II. Title. III. Series: Sautel, Anne, 1934- . Wombat Smith ; v. 2

PS8637.A82B44 2007   jC813'.6v   C2006-903938-0

Printed and bound in Canada.

To the memory of Fraser,
And to Rob,
Sara and Andrew.

– Anne Sautel

Chapter 1

Wombat picked up a pencil from the table where he was sitting and then stared down at the blank piece of paper in front of him. Then, before starting to write, he picked up another piece of paper that was completely covered with words. Although he had read them before, he read all the words again.

"It's from my friend Joshua," Wombat said as he showed the letter to Sandalfoot, even though the dog wouldn't understand. "I'd be able to write a whole page of exciting words too, if I belonged to a soccer team like Joshua does," he explained. "I'd be able to play better and win some games just like Joshua. Then I'd have something interesting to write about, instead of just playing ball with you." Then, for fear he had hurt Sandalfoot's feelings, he added quickly, "*And* with the boys in the neighborhood."

Wombat sighed as he put the letter down and moved the blank paper closer. He had just begun to write "Dear Joshua," when his sister Mary came into the kitchen.

"I have something for you," Mary said as she stood beside the table where Wombat was

sitting. "It's something very special," she added, holding it out of sight behind her back.

"A chocolate cookie?" Wombat asked hopefully.

"Better than that," Mary replied.

I can't think of anything better than a chocolate cookie, Wombat thought to himself. *Unless it's a cookie with chocolate chips.* "I know!" he guessed after thinking about it again. "It's a chocolate cookie with chocolate chips in it."

"No," Mary said impatiently. Unable to wait any longer, she thrust an envelope toward him. "It's a letter."

"It's from Tasmania!" Wombat exclaimed in surprise, for when he saw the postmark, he knew it was another letter from Joshua.

As Mary waited, Wombat read the letter quietly to himself. "Joshua's going with his team to the soccer camp in China – just like he'd hoped," Wombat said, remembering that Joshua had written about it in another letter.

"It's not Joshua's team," Mary corrected him. "It's the coach's team." She knew that Joshua had joined the soccer team coached by their father's friend in Tasmania.

Wombat ignored Mary as he continued to read. "He can ask a friend to go with the team to Beijing," he said excitedly. "And he wonders if *I* want to be that friend."

"If you go to China, I want to go too," Mary said.

"Wombat's not going anywhere," their mother said, entering the kitchen. "But you are going back to school for the afternoon," she said to Mary.

As soon as Mary and Mrs. Smith left the kitchen, Wombat put Joshua's letter in his pocket. *I can't mention I want to go to China*, he thought sadly. *My mother would worry too much if I went there.* He remembered how worried she had been when he went back to Tasmania where he had been all alone as a baby before becoming a member of the Smith family.

Mrs. Smith did not ask about China when she walked back into the kitchen after taking Mary to school. Instead, after asking Wombat if he wanted a glass of milk, she mixed some powdered marsupial milk in a glass of water. "I'll have to get more sent from Australia soon," she said when she noticed it was almost gone, for Wombat wasn't able to drink cow's milk like Mary. "Have you thought what you would like to do this afternoon?" his mother asked, while she watched him drink the milk.

"I have thought I would like to go to the library," he said, for he wanted to learn about China if Joshua was going there, even though he couldn't go himself.

"That's a good idea, but be careful crossing the street," his mother reminded him. Then she gave him the money he would need for the bus and a chocolate cookie in case he became hungry.

The library wasn't far away, and he had just enough time to eat his cookie before the bus stopped in front of the building. As he left the bus, he waved goodbye to the driver, then skipped along the sidewalk, up the steps of the building, and through the door.

"What book would you like to look at today?" the librarian asked as Wombat climbed onto the chair beside her desk.

"I'd like to read about China," he said. Then, in case she did not understand, he spelled it for her. "And a book about Beijing," he added, taking Joshua's letter from his pocket to show her the word "Beijing" written there. She seemed so pleased when she saw the way Joshua had spelled it, that Wombat wished he was able to spell it too. And he decided right then that he would learn to spell "Beijing," just as soon as he had the time.

"Come with me," the librarian said. She led him to the children's section of the library and stopped in front of some shelves filled with books that all began with the letter C. Then she looked down at his short arms and legs. "The shelf with the books about China is very high, so you will need something to stand on," she said, and she moved the library ladder over to him.

"Be careful while you are standing on it," she warned, before returning to her desk.

Wombat was very careful with the ladder, not only when he was standing on it, as he had been told, but also when he was climbing up and down too. After getting the book he wanted, he sat on one of the rungs to look at the pictures.

There were photos of things he had never seen before, like tree peonies and Chinese plum blossoms, and raccoon dogs and civet cats. But the picture of a panda was the strangest one, he thought, for it wasn't at all like the large black-and-white stuffed animal that sat on Mary's bed. It wasn't much bigger than the neighbor's cat, and its face was more like a raccoon than a panda. It was called a "red panda," which was a very good name, he thought, since its fur was mostly red.

On the next page was a picture of the black-and-white giant panda that he recognized. And with it was the story of her birthday party at the Beijing Zoo. When Wombat read the date of the panda's birthday, he saw that it had been around this same time last year.

He carried the book to a nearby table where a woman was reading to a little girl. "Excuse me," he said politely, as he held up the panda's picture for her to see. "But do you know if a panda's birthday is on the same day every year?"

"Of course," she replied. "Everybody's birthday is on the same day every year."

That means the panda will have another party when Joshua is in China, Wombat thought, and he wished he could be there too.

Since the woman seemed to know a lot

about birthdays, he would have liked to ask her more about the panda's party. He wondered if there would be ice cream and a birthday cake. But he didn't want to interrupt her again, so he put the book down on the table and left the library without asking any more questions.

He had to wait a long time for the bus. When he finally got home, he greeted his mother and ate a cookie before going to his room. After reading Joshua's letter again, he thought about the time Joshua had looked after him while he was sick in Tasmania. The more he thought about Joshua, the more Wombat wished he could see him again.

"Dinner's ready," Mrs. Smith called, and Wombat hurried from his room to join the others at the table. "What did you learn at the library today?" Mrs. Smith asked, as Wombat scrambled onto the thick cushion on his chair.

"I learned that the pandas at the Beijing Zoo have birthday parties," Wombat replied.

"If Wombat goes to China, I want to go to the panda's party too," Mary said, watching Wombat as he ate some of his salad.

"Wombat's not going to China," Mr. Smith said. "Where did you get *that* idea?"

"From Joshua's letter," Mary said. "He wants Wombat to go to a soccer camp with him."

"And learn to speak Chinese," Wombat added, for Joshua had mentioned language lessons in his letter.

"May I see the letter?" Mr. Smith asked. Wombat handed it to him, but instead of reading it right then, Mr. Smith set it down on the table. "I'll read it later when we have finished eating and I've washed my hands," he explained.

When dinner was over, Wombat went sadly to his room to answer Joshua's letter. He crumpled up the letter he had started and took out a fresh piece of paper. "I can't go to China," he wrote. He thought for a minute or two, then continued. "If you go to the panda's party, please tell her happy birthday for me."

If I don't go to China, I might never see Joshua again, he thought sadly. And he decided right then that even though he had told Joshua he wouldn't be going, he would still try to find a way to get to China.

Chapter 2

For the next two weeks, Wombat thought about ways to remind his parents that he wanted to go to China. He tried drawing pictures of things he remembered from the book about China he had seen at the library, and he took the panda from Mary's bed so that he could sit it at the dinner table. He suggested they have Chinese food one night and hoped that the fortune inside his cookie would say he should go to China. But the fortune on the paper read, "To find that which is lost is to have good luck," which didn't make any sense since he hadn't lost anything.

I would like good luck, he admitted, but he wished it had mentioned China. If he had known how to make fortune cookies, he could have put a fortune about China in all the cookies, and he decided right then that he would learn to make fortune cookies, just as soon as he had the time.

But his parents didn't seem to understand any of his hints. And since he had never learned to hint, he wondered if he was doing something wrong. Then he remembered the "how-to" books at the library, and he wished he'd asked the librarian for a "how to hint" book when he was there.

Then another letter came from Joshua, replying to the letter that Wombat had sent. "I'm sorry you're not coming to the soccer camp," Joshua's letter began. "I was looking forward to seeing you again. Maybe we'll get another chance someday."

There's never going to be another chance, Wombat thought sadly. And he felt even more unhappy than before.

Then one morning, his mother woke him as she entered his room. "Your father and I read the letter from Joshua that you gave us," she began.

"And we have decided that you should go to the soccer camp."

"We didn't want to tell you until we were sure you could go," Mr. Smith said, following Mrs. Smith into the room. "I just heard back from the camp director. One of the boys had to leave, and with the team short a player, the boys won't be able to play in the soccer match. That is why everyone needs you to join the team, even though there will only be one week left to practice when you arrive."

"After we drop you off, we can take Mary to see some places in Beijing," Mrs. Smith added. "We'll pick you up when the camp's over and bring you home."

"We'll be leaving for China next week," Mr. Smith announced as he and Mrs. Smith left the room.

Am I really going to China? Wombat wondered as he sat up, suddenly wide awake. *Am I really going to see Joshua again? And do the boys really need me on their soccer team?* Because he wanted it all so badly, he was afraid it had only been a dream.

✳✳✳

But it was true, and after a week that seemed very long, the day for the trip arrived. As Wombat and his family rode in the taxi that was taking them to the airport, he became more and more excited, and then finally they were on the plane.

When they found their seats, Mr. Smith sat beside Wombat, and Mrs. Smith sat with Mary in the seats directly in front of them. Wombat looked at the other passengers who walked by in the aisle and watched as they put their luggage in the compartments over their seats. Then he watched the activity on the airstrip until the plane left the runway and they were in the air at last, on their way to China.

As soon as the message came that the seat-belts could be undone, Mary knelt on her seat to hand Wombat a book she had brought from school. Before he had time to look at it, Wombat saw a flight attendant with a cart stop beside their seats.

After giving a cup of tea to Mrs. Smith and a glass of milk to Mary, the attendant turned to Wombat. "Would you like a glass of milk too?" she asked.

"I'd like a glass of marsupial milk, please," he replied.

She looked at Wombat as though she did not understand. "There's whole milk or one percent or two percent," she said finally.

"Thank you, but just regular marsupial milk will be fine," Wombat replied, for although he had learned how to add and subtract, he didn't know anything about percents.

The attendant stared at him. "There's regular one percent and regular two percent and regular whole," she said. "There's no regular marsupial."

"Then I'll have orange juice, please," Wombat said. *But it's very strange*, he thought, *that an airplane going everywhere would not have every kind of milk for everyone.* He would have mentioned it to the pilot if he had understood percents, and he decided right then that he would learn about percents, just as soon as he had the time.

After awhile, a movie was shown, and even though Wombat had seen it once before, he was glad to have something to do since the trip was very long. When the movie was over and he had eaten some food, he was very tired and began to fall asleep.

I wonder if Joshua looks the same, he

thought sleepily, for he hadn't seen his friend in a very long time.

But I don't look the same! he realized, suddenly remembering the way he had looked in Tasmania with his feverish eyes and runny nose. He was wide awake. *How will Joshua know it's me when he isn't expecting to see me there?* he wondered. He thought about his letter to Joshua and the one that Joshua had written back. And Wombat wished now that he hadn't hurried to send the letter in time for Joshua to get it.

Chapter 3

It was afternoon in China on the day they arrived. They didn't have any trouble finding Mr. Lee, one of the camp directors, at the airport, for he was holding up a sign with the name "Smith" written on it. He took them to his car, and as they drove through Beijing, Wombat and Mary were surprised to see the large number of people riding bicycles in the midst of the cars on the crowded streets.

As they came closer to the camp, Wombat began to feel excited. But when Mr. Lee parked the car in front of the building that was being used as a dormitory for the boys, Wombat began to worry again that Joshua wouldn't remember him.

Mr. Lee led the Smiths inside and up the stairs to the bedrooms on the second floor. "This will be your room for the week you are with us," he said to Wombat as he knocked on a closed door halfway down the hall. The door was opened right away by a boy in a soccer uniform, and Mr. Lee introduced him. "This is Jordon Matthews. He is here from England. And this is

Wombat, your new roommate," Mr. Lee explained to the boy. "And Mr. and Mrs. Smith, and Mary."

"My other roommate had to leave, so I'll be glad to have company again," the boy said as he looked curiously at Mr. and Mrs. Smith and Mary and then back at Wombat again. "And everyone else is going to be happy too. Now we'll have enough players for a team, so we can be in the big game."

"Please show Wombat around the camp," Mr. Lee said to the boy. "I will be taking Mr. and Mrs. Smith to the office to finish making the arrangements."

"Everyone calls me Matt," the boy said as he led Wombat from the room and down the hall. "It's short for Matthews."

"Everyone calls me Wombat," Wombat said. "It's short for Wombat Smith."

"Isn't 'Smith' the name of the people who brought you here?" Matt asked, looking confused.

"Yes. That's their name because they're my mother and father," Wombat explained. "And Mary is my sister, so her name is Smith too."

"I wouldn't have asked," Matt said, "but you don't look like them."

"No," Wombat admitted, and he suddenly felt strangely embarrassed. "I only look like me."

They arrived at the soccer field, and as Wombat looked at the boys who were exercising there, he wondered which one was Joshua. Dressed in their uniforms, like the one Matt was wearing, they all looked very much alike. Finally, when he looked more closely, Wombat was sure he saw Joshua. But as he watched, he noticed how well the boys all played together, and he knew he wouldn't be able to keep up with them.

"I'm going to go practice now," Matt said. "If you want to stay and watch, I can show you around later."

"Thank you," Wombat began, but then he thought he might be asked to play too if he stayed. *If they see me play, they'll know I'm not any good*, he thought. *And then nobody will be glad I'm here.* "Thank you," he said again, "but I'd like to go back to the room."

Inside the building, Wombat saw his family waiting with the director. They all went to the room Wombat had been assigned, and after Mr. Lee gave Wombat a soccer uniform to wear the next day, he left. Mrs. Smith opened a bag containing sandwiches she had bought at the airport, knowing they would all be too tired to eat a proper dinner. When all the food was gone, it was time for Mr. and Mrs. Smith and Mary to go to their hotel.

"You will need some money while you are here," Mr. Smith said, handing Wombat a bag of coins. Wombat looked at the coins, which had the numbers one and five on one side and flowers engraved on the other. He was surprised by the amount of money he had been given.

"It's not as much as it seems," Mr. Smith

explained. "Yuan (Yu-awn) coins aren't worth the same as the money you are used to."

Mrs. Smith gave Wombat a pouch attached to a belt that he was to wear around his waist. "You can keep the coins in here so they don't get lost," she said, and she warned Wombat to always stay with the other boys so he wouldn't get lost either.

Mary gave him a postcard with a picture of a giant panda. "I bought this for you at the airport to keep in your knapsack. You are supposed to write your name and the address of the camp on it, in case you do get lost," she explained, and then she leaned closer to whisper. "It was Mother's idea, not mine. But *I* picked out the picture."

After they left, Wombat sat dejectedly on his bed. He was never going to belong here, he was certain of that. He could see that the boys were already a group of close friends and they wouldn't want someone new joining them – except maybe a friend of Joshua.

But Joshua probably won't remember me. Even if he does, he's not going to want anyone to know he's my friend when he sees I can't play soccer like the other boys. Suddenly

Wombat wished he could have gone with his family. *But Matt doesn't think I belong with my family either*, he thought sadly. But he was so tired from the long trip that by the time Matt returned to the room, Wombat had cried himself to sleep.

Chapter 4

Although Wombat slept soundly that night, he was still strangely tired the next morning. As he got out of bed, he found a note from Matt saying he had gone to the soccer field.

Excitedly, Wombat put on the soccer uniform that Mr. Lee had given him. *Maybe now I'll be more like Joshua and the other boys*, he thought. And he rushed to the full-length mirror that hung on the back of the door.

"Oh no!" he cried out loud. Instead of looking like the other boys' uniforms, it hung down his legs like a dress. *Of course it has to be extra-large*, he thought sadly, remembering that his shape was very different from that of the other boys. *A smaller one would never reach around my stomach or cover up my bottom.*

Before he could change back into his own clothes, there was a knock at the door. He did not want anyone to see him, so he waited, hoping the person would go away. But the knock came again, so he went to the door and opened it. There, standing in the hall in front of him, was Joshua.

"Wombat!" Joshua exclaimed, stepping into the room.

"Hello, Joshua," Wombat said nervously.

"Is it really you?" And Joshua ran to Wombat to hug him.

"Yes," Wombat replied. "It really is!"

"I can't believe you're here!" Joshua said.

"I can't believe it too," Wombat agreed.

"But I'm glad you are," Joshua quickly added. He looked down shyly at his feet.

"Yes," Wombat said happily. "Now I'm glad too."

They both looked at the floor without saying anything. Finally Joshua spoke. "I was going to go to breakfast with Matt, but I will go with you instead." He led Wombat from the room without asking why Wombat's uniform looked like a dress.

As soon as they entered the dining room, Wombat was greeted enthusiastically by all the boys. They explained how important it was that he had joined the team, for if they won the soccer match, they'd get the chance to go to another camp next year.

"And if we're picked to go, my coach back home can go with us," Joshua added excitedly.

Oh, Wombat thought nervously, for he did not want to disappoint any of them, especially their coach who was his father's friend.

"It was only because of our coach that I was allowed to come here," Joshua explained to Wombat as they walked to the soccer field after breakfast. "He talked my father into letting me leave the farm to come with the team." He paused as he waved at Matt and the other boys who were already on the soccer field. "I like playing soccer," he added. "But I've found that I like helping at the animal hospital even more. We were all asked if we wanted to help, but I was the only one who signed up for it. I guess that makes me even more lucky to be here."

"I'm lucky to be here too," Wombat said.

After meeting Mr. Chang, the coach, Wombat joined the others on the field. He was told to play midfield, and he hurried to stand behind Joshua, who was one of the forwards. Matt took his position as goalkeeper and the boys began to kick the ball up and down the field. Wombat ran as quickly as he could, but with his short legs and long uniform, he wasn't able to keep up with them.

Then Wombat saw the ball coming toward him. *Now's my chance*, he thought excitedly. *I'll kick it as hard as I can so it will go all the way down the field.* But as he tried to swing his leg, the long uniform held it down. With the small kick, he only grazed the ball, and it rolled a short distance away from his foot.

Looking up quickly, he noticed two of his teammates who were standing a short distance away whispering to each other. *Now they don't want me here*, he thought, for he was sure they were complaining about the way he had played. *But if I'd had a proper uniform, I might have been able to kick the ball better.*

"There will be four more days of practices before the Beijing boy's team comes to play in the soccer match," Mr. Chang informed them when the game was over. "You all need more practice kicking the ball if you hope to win, for they are a very good team." Then before Wombat had a chance to leave the field with the others, Mr. Chang stopped him. "You haven't played much soccer, have you?" he asked.

"Not *very* much," Wombat admitted. "Never in a soccer match. And never in a dress."

The coach stared for a minute at Wombat's uniform. "We will have to do something about that," he said. "Your uniform will have to be stitched shorter before you play tomorrow."

Wombat hurried to where Joshua was waiting for him near the field. "I'll never be able to play soccer like the rest of you," Wombat complained as they went to get their lunch.

"Don't worry," Joshua assured him. "You'll be better after more practice, you'll see."

But if I don't get better, I might not be able to help win the game, worried Wombat, even though Joshua had told him not to.

When the boys finished eating, they went to a classroom for their language lesson. Wombat walked up to the teacher at the front of the room while the others went to their desks.

"I am Miss Lo," she said, greeting him with a smile. "I am pleased that you are joining our class."

"I am pleased too," Wombat said. "I've wanted to learn to speak Chinese."

"The language you will be learning is called Mandarin," Miss Lo explained. Then she indicated the desk at the front of the class where Wombat was to sit. "But before you sit down, you should introduce yourself to the class."

"I'm Wombat Smith," he said, shifting his feet with embarrassment as he remembered his badly fitting uniform.

"If you were Chinese, you would write your name 'Smith Wombat,'" Miss Lo explained. "Our family names are put first."

After Wombat sat down at the desk, she continued. "It is important to know that a word can mean several things. It's the pronunciation

of the word that gives it different meanings." She walked to the blackboard and picked up a piece of chalk. "Wombat, the class has been choosing words they would like to learn in Mandarin. Can you think of a special word you would like to say?"

"'Cookie,'" Wombat answered without having to think at all.

"The Mandarin word for 'cookie' is 'bĭng' (be-ung)," Miss Lo explained, writing it down on the blackboard. "That's a good word," she added with a smile.

"Yes," Wombat agreed. "It *is* a good word."

When class was over for the day, Wombat walked with Joshua and Matt to the soccer field to practice kicking the ball before dinner. "Did you pick any words to learn?" he asked them.

"I picked 'soccer.' 'Zú'" (zoo), Matt replied.

"And I picked 'animal.' 'Wù'" (woo), Joshua said. "I use that word all the time at the animal hospital."

"Those are good words too," Wombat said.

After spending more time talking with Joshua when dinner was over, Wombat began to feel sleepy. As soon as the coach had taken his uniform away to have it sewn, Wombat crawled into bed. "Bǐng" (be-ung), he said aloud as he thought about the word he had learned, and he practiced it several more times so he wouldn't forget. But he wondered if he should have chosen a more important word, like the name of the camp or the camp's telephone number – the things he had forgotten to write on the panda postcard Mary had given him.

No. There really isn't a better word than "cookie," he decided, after thinking about it very carefully. *But if I had to pick another word, I think it would be "chocolate."*

As he began to fall asleep, he suddenly remembered that the camp schedule had mentioned that the field trip to the Beijing Zoo would be the next day. It was the one thing he had really wanted to do after seeing the picture of the giant panda in the book at the library. But even though he was excited about going to the panda's party, he could not stop thinking about having to play in the soccer practice in the morning.

What if my uniform isn't shortened in time? And even if it is shortened, my legs won't be any longer, he thought sadly. Then he remembered that Matt practiced every morning. *If Matt can practice kicking the ball before breakfast, so can I*, he thought. And he decided right then that he would get up early every morning starting the very next day. But he wondered if he could get good enough in just four days to help his team win the game.

Chapter 5

Wombat was thankful when Mr. Chang brought the hemmed uniform to his room early enough so he could go to the soccer field in the morning. He kicked the ball for a while, and by the time he went in for breakfast, he thought he was better than he'd been the day before. When breakfast was over, he returned to the field with the others and kicked the ball a few more times before the practice game.

"You're playing better today," Matt said, and since Matt seemed to know a lot about soccer, Wombat felt very pleased.

"It must have been your long uniform yesterday that kept you from running fast," Joshua said when Wombat ran to his place midfield behind him. And Wombat was happy that Joshua, too, had noticed his improvement.

Soon after the game had started, one of the players on the other team kicked the ball out-of-bounds. Since Wombat happened to be nearby, he was told to throw the ball back onto the field. But he found that his arms weren't long enough to lift the ball over his head and it hit his forehead. By leaning his head down, out of the way, he was able to raise the ball high enough, but because he was facing the ground, he couldn't see where to throw it.

Everyone's waiting for the ball, he thought nervously. He quickly looked up at the field and threw the ball as hard as he could. But instead of it going to one of his teammates, the ball bounced off the back of his head and onto the ground.

"You'll throw better after more practice," Mr. Chang said, noticing Wombat's embarrassment. Then he picked up the ball and motioned Wombat onto the field before throwing it to him.

Wombat felt a little better after the coach's words, until he walked past two boys who were talking, and overheard one of them mention his name. Then he heard the other boy remark that Joshua should not have asked Wombat to join their team.

Nobody wants me here, Wombat thought sadly. *And Joshua won't either after he loses all his friends because of me.*

While they were on the bus that afternoon on the way to the zoo, Wombat worried that Joshua would hear what the boy had said. However, all of the boys were excited about the field trip and talked only about the panda's birthday. Wombat became excited too when he remembered that Mary had wanted to go to the party as well.

"Maybe I'll see my family there!" Wombat said to Joshua.

"Then I'll be able to meet them," Joshua replied.

"Yes," Wombat said hesitantly. He remembered how upset he'd been when Matt thought he was different from his family, and he didn't want Joshua to think so too.

When they arrived at the zoo, Mr. Lee bought their tickets at the entrance, and since the panda's party would not begin for some time, they went to the tiger hill and the monkey hall first.

"Look!" Joshua said pointing at the word "wù" (woo) on a sign for the golden monkeys. "That's 'animal,' my word from the language class." Then he looked at the other word "bin wei" (bing way). "I've seen that at the animal hospital, but I don't remember what it means."

"That's the word for 'endangered,'" Mr. Lee explained. "It means that these monkeys are becoming few in number, and if we don't look after them, they may all be gone one day."

They left the monkeys and walked toward the pandas. As they got closer, they could hear people calling to each other. Thinking the party had already begun, they hurried toward the giant panda enclosure, but they found that the shouting was coming from where the red pandas were kept. There were two red pandas inside the enclosure. One was as small as a little cat, and the larger one appeared to be its mother. The older panda was pacing as though disturbed while the little one followed behind her.

"I don't see why they're called pandas when they don't look like the other pandas at all," Matt exclaimed.

And Wombat wondered if Matt had thought that he shouldn't be called a Smith when he didn't look like the other Smiths in his family.

"Their favorite food is bamboo, just like the giant pandas," Mr. Lee explained. "That is why they are called pandas."

"My favorite foods are cookies and cake," Wombat said to Matt. "Just like my sister Mary."

A woman who had been searching in the piles of bamboo came out of the panda enclosure and began looking. When she came close to where the boys were standing, Joshua approached her.

"Why is the big panda upset?" he asked.

The woman indicated that she didn't speak English, so Mr. Lee repeated Joshua's question in Mandarin.

"One of her young is missing," Mr. Lee explained to the boys, translating the woman's answer. "Hong Lu, the twin of the other little panda, somehow got out. Her mother doesn't know where she is."

"But she's endangered too," Wombat said, pointing to the word "bin wei" on the sign that was there.

"Yes," Mr. Lee said. "We must hope she will be found by someone who knows she is an animal protected by the law, and that he would be punished if he kept her or tried to sell her to someone else."

Why would anyone want to keep Hong Lu away from her mother? Wombat wondered, and he felt sad for the little panda, remembering how he had felt when he was lost in Tasmania.

They walked to the giant panda's enclosure and found that a crowd had already gathered there. Soon a cake arrived in a large bowl, which was placed in front of the animal.

I hope the panda doesn't mind if I sing "Happy Birthday" in English, Wombat thought. He wished he'd learned to sing it in Mandarin before coming to the party, and he decided right then that he would learn to sing the Chinese birthday song, just as soon as he had the time.

Wombat was glad when he saw the plates filled with small pieces of birthday cake being passed among the crowd. He hoped this cake would be chocolate and not bamboo, for although he'd never eaten a bamboo cake, he didn't think that he would like it. It wasn't made of bamboo, he discovered, but when he took a bite he found it was mostly fruit, almost like the Christmas cake he had tasted once. *This might be all right at Christmastime*, he thought, *but it's not the birthday-time cake I would have liked.* And as he thought about all the cakes and all the cookies he had ever tasted, he suddenly remembered the fortune cookie.

Of course! What I have to do is find something that is lost so that I can get good luck, he thought. *And when I share my luck with the other boys and we win the game, they'll be glad that Joshua asked me to join the team.*

"Joshua, we have to find Hong Lu," he whispered excitedly. "Then we'll have good luck for the game."

"What makes you think that a panda will bring us luck?" Joshua asked.

"A cookie," replied Wombat. "That's what made me think of it."

Without explaining anything else, Wombat began to look around at the people in the crowd. Suddenly, in the distance, he saw his mother and father. He knew Mary would be there too, even though she was hidden by all the people. He wanted to run to them and hug them and say he missed them, but if he did, he would have to introduce them to all the boys.

And my family would find out I'm not good enough to play soccer with the others on the team, he thought. *And the boys would think the same as Matt – that I don't belong with the others in my family.* Because he worried about what

everyone would think, he decided not to go to his family after all. But as he began to turn away, he saw his mother look in his direction. He stepped in front of Mr. Lee quickly, and he remained hidden until it was time to leave the zoo.

Later that night, as he lay awake in bed, he could not stop thinking about his family. *What if my mother saw me?* he thought. He knew how hurt she would be if she realized that he was trying to hide from her. *What will I do if I see her again tomorrow at the Forbidden City?* he wondered guiltily, as he thought about the field trip he would be taking the next day. And because he didn't know if he would hide from her again, he felt even more ashamed than he had before.

Chapter 6

After the soccer practice the next day, the boys took the bus to the Forbidden City. They went through the gate into the large open square filled with visitors like themselves, where the splendor of the golden roofs could be seen beyond the walls. And while Wombat looked at the interesting sculptures of lions and dragons inside the walls, he thought of nothing else. He forgot about his worry of seeing his family again and of the soccer game. And for a while he forgot his hope of finding Hong Lu. It was only when he and Joshua entered the palace

garden filled with trees and flowers that he was reminded of the little panda.

"Maybe Hong Lu is here," Wombat said, for he remembered the book in the library that said pandas liked to climb trees.

But although they looked carefully in every tree and bush beside the path of colored stones, there was no sign of the little panda. Finally, they had to give up their search, for it was time to leave the Forbidden City.

There's no time left to find Hong Lu now, Wombat thought as he rode on the bus back to camp. And he wondered what he could do to help his team win with only one day left before the game.

***

A field trip to one of the old districts of the city had been planned for the following morning. The soccer match was to take place the day after that, and since they would be back by dinnertime, the final practice would be in the evening. Although Wombat would have liked more time to practice, he joined the others eagerly as they climbed onto the bus.

"Here you will see how some of the people in Beijing live," Mr. Lee said as he drove the bus through the narrow streets.

After Mr. Lee parked, the boys got out and walked along a street lined with shops where people rode past on bicycles. Some pulled carts to carry all their purchases, while others pulled a covered seat, large enough to carry two or three people, which Mr. Lee called a rickshaw. The boys wanted to divide into smaller groups so they could go into different stores, and Mr. Lee gave them his permission. He told everyone to meet him in front of a restaurant that had a large sign, which could be seen from a long distance down the street.

"You must stay with a teammate," he cautioned. "And remember, many people in this district do not speak English. For safety, do not leave this section of the street. We must all remain in the same area, so that no one gets lost."

The boys divided into twos and threes, and Wombat went with Joshua into a store where they each bought a cap with the Chinese char-acter for "Beijing" written in thread above the visor. Then they looked at the other shops on the street, but Wombat didn't see anything else he wanted to buy, until they came to a store that sold fruit and nuts. They went inside and Wombat looked at all the food, but because he couldn't make up his mind, he had to look at everything again.

"Jingdongs?" the woman asked finally, holding up a nut to show him.

"Yes, please," Wombat answered, and then he repeated "Yes" in Mandarin. "Wei" (way), he said, pronouncing it as he had learned in class. "And wei," he said again, pointing to some red goji berries, which he thought looked good to eat, even though he had never tasted them before.

She handed him a bag of both, and after Wombat had chosen a couple of white pears and a honey peach, the woman picked up a frame from the counter and began moving rows of beads up and down the rods attached inside.

"That's an abacus," Joshua whispered. "We learned about it in class. It's for doing arithmetic, like adding and subtracting."

"I've never seen beads that add and subtract before," Wombat remarked in amazement, and he wondered if they could do percents as well. He thought he would like to have beads that do arithmetic for him, and he decided right

then that he would learn to use an abacus, just as soon as he had the time.

After he had paid for the nuts and fruit, Wombat still had a few coins left, and as he wondered what else he could buy, he remembered the word for "cookie" he had learned in language class.

"Bǐng" (be-ung)? he asked, pronouncing the word very carefully.

"Bǐng?" the woman repeated, sounding surprised. But she went into a room at the back of the shop and returned quickly with a small paper bag in her hand. "Bǐng," she said again, and after giving it to Wombat, she took the rest of his money.

Wombat left the shop with Joshua and waved to Mr. Lee in front of the restaurant. Wombat was so interested in looking in the store windows as they continued down the street, that he did not see the bicycle and cart parked on the sidewalk in front of him.

Suddenly he tripped and fell, landing on top of the cart.

"Are you all right?" Joshua asked as he rushed to help Wombat stand up.

"Some of me is," Wombat replied. "But

some of me isn't." He showed Joshua the toes he had stubbed.

"I'll get Mr. Lee," said Joshua, looking back in the direction where the camp director had been standing. But they had walked too far to see Mr. Lee or any of their teammates in the crowded street.

"My toes will feel better if they rest for a minute," Wombat said, for he did not want the boys to know that his legs were not only short, but clumsy as well.

There wasn't anywhere to sit on the busy street, so Joshua helped Wombat onto one of the side streets. A lot of people were there too, so they turned down another narrow street, and then another. Finally, they came to a quiet place where they could sit without being disturbed.

"Do you have anything in there to help your foot?" Joshua asked, pointing to the knapsack Wombat had put down on the ground beside him.

"No," Wombat said as he looked inside, for he had taken most of his things out and left them in his room at the camp. "But something to eat would help a little." And after giving one of the jingdong nuts to Joshua, he took one for himself.

This almost has a Christmas taste too, like the panda's birthday cake, Wombat thought, for he was reminded of the chestnuts he had roasted one Christmas in the fireplace at home.

"We're not going to get back to the meeting place in time," Joshua said, after they had sat there for a while. "And I'm supposed to help at the animal hospital this afternoon." But when Wombat had trouble standing on his foot, Joshua knew they wouldn't get very far. "Wait here," he said. "I'll be back as soon as I find Mr. Lee."

At first Wombat didn't mind being left alone, for the street was quiet without any traffic. He realized he felt hungry, and after eating both pears and the honey peach, he remembered the cookie he had bought.

Maybe it's a fortune cookie, he thought, and before taking it from the bag, he began to think of all the different fortunes that he would like. Finally, he decided on the one he wanted the most. "Please tell me that my toes will get better soon and not hurt so much," he whispered into the bag. Then, so the cookie would know he wasn't just thinking of himself, he quickly added, "That's so I can practice for the game."

But when he took the cookie from the bag, he was disappointed to find there wasn't any fortune after all, for it was just a plain cookie with an almond on the top. He slowly nibbled around the edge of the cookie and by the time he came to the nut in the center, he began to worry that Joshua hadn't been able to find Mr. Lee.

Maybe I won't get back in time for the soccer practice, he thought. And he began to worry that his foot wouldn't be better in time to play in the soccer match. Even though the boys were unhappy with the way he played, it would be worse if he didn't play at all. And he examined his hurt toes, wondering if he would be able to walk by himself to the meeting place.

Chapter 7

In case Joshua was on his way back, Wombat decided to wait awhile before trying to find the restaurant where he was supposed to meet Mr. Lee and the other boys. Soon he began to worry that it was getting very late in the morning, and all he had left for his lunch were some berries. He was just about to look in the bag when he heard a sound close by.

It wasn't very loud – just some quiet snorts, and then the snorts became squeaks. When the animal was close enough to sniff the bag of fruit, Wombat slowly turned his head. And he recognized the same red fur he had seen at the zoo.

It's Hong Lu! he thought. He was so excited that he wanted to put his arms around her and tell her not to worry anymore, for he was going to take her back to her mother. *But that will frighten her*, he realized, *and then she'll run away and get lost again.* As he sat very still beside the small animal, he remembered the fortune cookie. *After I take Hong Lu back to her home*, he thought happily, *I will take the good luck back to the team.*

He knew he had to make friends with the

panda first before trying to pick her up. He took some goji berries from his knapsack and squeezed them in his hand. When the little panda finished licking the red juice from his fur, she curled up in Wombat's lap with her large bushy tail around her. After putting the remaining berries in his knapsack with the jingdong nuts, Wombat stood up with Hong Lu in his arms. He limped slowly, turning onto one narrow street after another, but nothing looked familiar. He hadn't gone very far when he realized he was lost.

Just as his foot became too sore to walk any farther, he saw a rickshaw parked on the street. Even though he didn't have any money, Wombat hurried over, hoping to get a ride to where he was to meet the boys. The driver wasn't there, but as Wombat turned to walk away, he saw a man running toward him from a nearby house. Thankful that the driver had returned, Wombat smiled as he went to meet him.

"May I have a ride, please?" Wombat asked. But before Wombat could explain that he would have to pay him later, the man motioned for Wombat to follow him back to the house.

At first Wombat was glad the rickshaw driver was friendly, but as he got closer to the front door, he stopped. He had never seen this man before, and he knew he should never go anywhere with a stranger. After opening the door, the man called out a name, and a woman appeared immediately in the doorway. She greeted Wombat with a smile and hurried closer to stroke Hong Lu's back. The man called another name, and a younger woman ran from the house speaking excitedly when she saw the panda.

"Hong Lu," Wombat explained, holding the panda up so they could see her better. "She's the panda from the zoo."

But they shook their heads, and Wombat realized they didn't understand English. *I should try to say something in Mandarin*, he thought, but the only word he could remember was the word for "cookie."

"Bĭng" (be-ung), he said. He thought he must have said it well, for the younger woman hurried into the house and returned a minute later with a cookie. "Thank you," he said politely, and he took it from her even though he had not really meant to ask for it.

But as Wombat looked down at the cookie, the man rushed toward him, and then both women lunged at him too. *They must want the cookie!* Wombat thought in surprise. But when he tried to hand it back, instead of taking the cookie, they tried to grab Hong Lu.

"No! It's against the law," Wombat cried, realizing that they thought he was giving them

the panda. "You can't keep her for a pet." And he wished he could remember the Mandarin word for "endangered" that he had seen on the sign at the zoo.

The man reached out and grabbed Hong Lu by the tail. Startled, she extended her claws as far as they would go, and hissing, lashed out with her paw. As the man jumped backward to avoid being scratched, the two women stepped back as well.

Wombat knew that this was his only chance to escape. He began to limp away on his sore foot as quickly as he could. There would only be a few seconds before the man recovered from his surprise, and then it wouldn't be long before he and Hong Lu were caught.

Chapter 8

Wombat hobbled away from the house with Hong Lu in his arms as the man and the two women chased him. They had almost caught up, when Wombat came to the rickshaw again. He knew that this was his only chance to escape.

He jumped onto the bicycle seat and began to ride slowly down the street, unsure of where he was going. The bicycle wobbled at first as Wombat pedalled unevenly to protect his sore foot. As he began to go faster, Hong Lu looked over his shoulder at the man and

women running behind them. *They think I'm stealing the rickshaw,* Wombat realized suddenly, and he became more frightened as other people on the street began shouting and running after him.

Then two motorcycles joined the chase, and as they pulled up beside him, Wombat saw they were driven by two policemen. They waved at him to stop, and one of the men said something in Mandarin.

"I don't understand," Wombat said, shaking his head.

"You will get down from there," the other policeman said, speaking in English.

As Wombat climbed off the bicycle, the man and two women caught up to him. They talked excitedly to the policemen, pointing at Hong Lu in Wombat's arms. Then the two women climbed into the rickshaw, and the man got on the bicycle and took them away.

"You will come with us," the policeman said to Wombat, speaking more brusquely than before.

"Are you taking me back to the soccer camp?" asked Wombat. He hoped the policemen knew the way, for he had forgotten to write the address on the panda postcard in his knapsack.

"No," the policeman replied. "We are taking you to jail."

"I can't go to jail!" Wombat said nervously. "I have to go back to the camp."

"You can go in five years, when you are out of jail," the policeman said.

"Five years!" Wombat exclaimed, for he could not believe what he was hearing.

"Not only did you steal a rickshaw," the policeman explained, "but you took the panda from the zoo."

"No, you don't understand!" Wombat cried. "I didn't take Hong Lu. I found her on the road when I was sitting with my toes." And he held up his foot to show the policeman where it hurt. "I didn't *steal* the rickshaw. I was going to give it back."

"The man said you wanted to give him the panda for a cookie," the policeman continued. "Then you stole his rickshaw so you could get away before he reported you."

"But I didn't want the cookie," Wombat pleaded. "And it was only my toes that wanted the rickshaw." As he began to hold up his foot again, a police car drove up and stopped beside them. The driver got out and joined the other two policemen. He reached out to take Hong Lu, but stepped back quickly when she lashed out at him.

The policeman who spoke English turned to Wombat. "You will look after the panda in the jail until the people from the zoo come for her," he said.

"Please," Wombat begged. "Can't we just wait here instead of going to jail?"

The policeman did not answer as he lifted Wombat and Hong Lu onto the back seat of the car. Then he climbed in beside them. The other two policemen got into the front, and after they had traveled down several streets, they stopped in front of a building. When they got out, two of the policemen ushered Wombat and Hong Lu through the front door to a desk where a guard was sitting. The policemen spoke to the guard in Mandarin and then left the building.

The guard stared at the panda for a minute, and then at Wombat. "Name?" he asked finally, speaking in English.

"Wombat," Wombat replied.

"What bat?" the man asked.

"I'm not any kind of bat," Wombat explained. "I'm a marsupial."

"Marsupial," repeated the guard as he wrote it down. "And what is your first name?"

"Wombat *is* my first name," Wombat answered nervously. And if his mouth hadn't been too dry to speak, he would have mentioned that his last name was Smith.

"Any jail records, Wombat Marsupial?" the guard asked, and Wombat shook his head. "Any fingerprints?"

"I don't know," Wombat answered, for he had never wondered if he had fingerprints before. He held up his hand so the man could look, but when he saw that it was still stained red from the berry juice, he quickly put it down again.

"You will have a special cell for now," the guard said. "After the people come for the panda, you will go to a cell with the other prisoners."

Wombat started to shake, and the fur around his mouth began to tremble. The guard paused to look at him more closely. "How old are you, Marsupial?" he asked.

Wombat thought for a moment, wondering if he should give his age in people years or dog years. Since he couldn't make up his mind, he decided to say both. "I'm two in Smith years, but fourteen in Sandalfoot's."

"What Smith? What foot?" the guard asked, seeming annoyed at being given two answers.

"I'm fourteen," Wombat said, quickly choosing only one answer. *But maybe the dogs in China don't count their age the same as Sandalfoot*, he thought suddenly. And not wanting the guard to get confused, he added, "But only if your dogs count their years in sevens."

"Sevens?" the man asked. Then without waiting for an answer, he called another guard over to the desk. "This guard does not speak English," he said to Wombat. "The guard who takes his place later will be able to speak with you."

"But if he can't speak English, how will he understand what I'm saying?" Wombat whimpered, as the guard hurried over to grab Wombat's knapsack away from him.

"Please give it back," Wombat begged, as the guard looked through the things inside. "There are only goji berries for the panda."

The man at the desk said something in Mandarin, and when the guard finished checking the bag, he handed it back. Then he led Wombat and Hong Lu down a hall and into a very private cell. As Wombat listened to the guard walk away, he set Hong Lu down and pulled on the cell door as hard as he could. "Please come back," he called. "I didn't steal anything. I want to go home!" After calling out a few more times, Wombat finally gave up and turned to look at the room.

The only furniture was a bed, a chair, and a small table. On the table, there was a vase holding a few dead flowers in a little water. Wombat removed the flowers and carried the vase to where he had left Hong Lu on the floor. She was very weak, having gone a long time without much food, and when Wombat poured a little water into his hand, she lapped it up thirstily, even though it was stale and must not have tasted very good.

"Never mind," Wombat said, lifting her onto his lap. "The men from the zoo will be here soon to take you back to your mother."

But no one's coming for me. No one even knows I'm here, he thought sadly. *But no one will like me if they find out I'm in jail. Not my family. Not Joshua. And not any of the boys on the team.* He began to cry quietly, and Hong Lu looked up at him as one of his tears fell onto the red fur on her head.

Chapter 9

Wombat sat on the floor of the jail cell, holding the little panda on his lap. As he waited for the men who would take her back to the zoo, he wondered if her mother would remember her. Then he recalled miserably that it would be five years before he could go home, and he wondered if his mother would remember him after such a long time.

"I wish I were you," he said, looking down at Hong Lu as he stroked her fur. "Then I would be taken to the zoo, and I could find a way out of there just like you did."

Then he noticed that his hand was red from the goji berries. *If I dye all my hair red, the men might think I'm a red panda too!* he thought excitedly. He grabbed the remaining goji berries, squeezed them in his hand, and rubbed the juice onto his head. But he soon realized that, just as he had needed an extra-large soccer uniform, he would need an extra-large bag of berries to get enough juice to cover himself.

No one will think I'm Hong Lu, even if all of me is red, he thought, for he knew his face was different from hers, and instead of having a

large, bushy tail, he hardly had any tail at all. *Maybe they would take another animal instead of a panda*, he thought suddenly. *But what if they can only take one?* And he decided he would have to hide Hong Lu. He looked quickly around the room. The two far corners of the room were very dark, he noticed. So dark that he could not be seen clearly if he lay in one of them.

Then from down the hall came a voice he did not recognize, and he knew that the new guard had arrived. Wombat listened to the sound of the footsteps of the old guard disappearing down the hall. When he was sure the old guard left the building, he took off his soccer uniform and shoved it in his knapsack. After hiding it in one of the dark corners of the room, he went to get Hong Lu.

"I'll have to leave you here," he whispered. He carried the limp panda to his knapsack and tried to make her comfortable on top of his clothes. "But don't worry. Before they take me out of the cell, I will find a way to let them know you are here so they will take you too." He wished that Hong Lu was strong enough to look up at him to show she understood.

He heard the sound of footsteps in the hallway, and he hurried to lie down in the other dark corner of the cell. He curled into a ball like Hong Lu would have done, keeping his face down so only the top of his head would be seen.

The new guard stepped inside the cell door and looked around. "Wombat Marsupial," he called. Then he shouted something in Mandarin, and two people hurried in.

Wombat held his breath as he heard footsteps coming toward him, but instead of picking him up, the people stood beside him and began to argue. Although Wombat did not understand what they were saying, he thought they must be disagreeing about taking him to the zoo. Then he heard them say "wù" (woo), and he recognized the Mandarin word for "animal" that Joshua had taught him. And he thought that perhaps they had been told animal instead of panda, just as he had hoped.

He heard something that sounded like a cage being set down beside him, and then a blanket was thrown on top of him. He was picked up and lowered into the cage, and he could feel himself being carried toward the cell door.

I'm almost free! he thought, and he held his breath in his excitement. He was just going to tell the people about Hong Lu when he realized he could not speak to them, after all. If he did, they would know he wasn't the animal they were supposed to take to the zoo. H would have to wait until he was free, he realized. Until then, he couldn't tell anyone about her.

Then he thought about how weak Hong Lu had seemed when he picked her up, and he knew she wouldn't be able to go much longer without food and water. *Even if I don't say anything, someone will find her soon,* he reassured himself. But he remembered the wilted flowers and the stale water in the vase, and he wondered how long they had been left there without anyone noticing.

He had to think quickly of some way to save her, for there wasn't much time. Wombat knew he was already at the door of the cell.

Chapter 10

When Wombat was sure he had been carried through the cell door into the hallway, he knew he had no choice. He had to tell the people from the zoo that they'd made a mistake taking him instead of the panda.

As he hesitated, still afraid to speak, an idea came to him. *I wouldn't have to say anything to them if Hong Lu made a sound and they heard her.* And instead of speaking with people words, he called out with panda sounds, hoping Hong Lu would answer.

He tried to imitate the squeaking sounds she had made when she first appeared on the road beside him. But his voice, muffled by the blanket, couldn't carry to where Hong Lu lay. But she had snorted too, he remembered, and he snorted as loud as he could. Then he snorted again and again.

Just as he was about to give up and tell the people about Hong Lu, he heard a little snort from the corner of the cell. But the sound was so weak, he was afraid no one had heard it.

Then he could feel himself turning, and to his relief, he realized the cage was being carried back into the cell. He was lowered to the floor and when the cage door opened, his knapsack was shoved inside. Wombat heard a soft squeak beside him, and he snorted back joyfully to let Hong Lu know he was there.

Before long, Wombat could smell the outside air as the cage was lifted into a car. After traveling a short distance, they were carried into another building, and the knapsack with Hong Lu was taken away to a room. Wombat was carried into another, where a man in a white coat pulled him from the cage and set him down on a hard tabletop.

The man lifted the blanket to look at Wombat. "I don't know what kind of creature this is," he said, speaking in English.

How embarrassing! Wombat thought, closing his eyes, for he wasn't used to being peeked at under a blanket without any clothes on.

"Isn't it the panda, Doctor?" asked a voice on the other side of the room.

Doctor! Then this must be a hospital, Wombat realized, opening his eyes again. Then he thought that the other person's voice sounded familiar. *Joshua? It is Joshua. Joshua is here!*

"The panda was brought here in a knapsack and was taken to the other room," the doctor replied.

"Will this animal be going to the zoo?" Joshua asked, walking closer to the table.

"I'll have to examine it first to make sure it's healthy," the doctor said as he secured the blanket around Wombat again. "I'll get something to make it sleepy so that I'll be able to get a good look. You don't need to stay here. You can go see the panda, if you'd like to. This animal won't get away."

Wombat waited until he heard the doctor leave the room, and then, as Joshua bent closer,

Wombat looked up at him from under the blanket. "Joshua," he whispered.

Joshua jumped back and stood staring at the blanket.

"Joshua," Wombat said a little louder.

Joshua moved back to the table and lifted the blanket away from Wombat's face. "Wombat?" he whispered in surprise.

"It's me," Wombat answered. "I don't have any clothes on."

"I was so worried about you!" Joshua sighed with relief. "I'm sorry I left you alone so long. It took me awhile to find my way back to the meeting place. And after I found Mr. Lee and we went back for you, you were gone." He spoke quickly and then paused for a moment, before continuing. "All the boys searched for you. And then Mr. Lee said we had to go back to camp to wait because it was getting late. He said the police would find you."

"They found half of me," Wombat said. "And they would have found the other half too, if I'd told them it was Smith."

"Did the police take your soccer uniform?" Joshua asked.

"No. I put it in my knapsack with Hong Lu," Wombat replied.

"That's right – you found the panda!" Joshua realized suddenly. "Hey, that means you'll get the good luck and we'll win the soccer game tomorrow. I hope there's enough luck to get you out of here before the doctor gets back," he added as he ran from the room to find Wombat's uniform.

Wombat hadn't thought about how much luck there would be. *The fortune cookie didn't look big enough to hold very much luck*, he thought. He added up all the luck it must have taken to escape from jail and get to Joshua. And then he knew! There couldn't be any luck left inside the little cookie. *And without luck, the doctor probably won't let me leave, even in my uniform*, he thought. And he remembered the trouble he'd had when he was trying to leave Tasmania.

It wasn't long before Joshua returned with the knapsack. Wombat was just going to tell him that the luck was gone, when he heard the doctor's footsteps coming toward the room.

"I'll talk to him in the hall while you get dressed. Then wait for me outside the building," Joshua said quickly before he left the room.

Wombat put on the uniform, which was rumpled and stained from the goji berries. Then he peeked nervously at the doctor before stepping into the hall. The doctor nodded politely as he walked past, and then turned away without saying anything. *He doesn't think I'm any different from the other boys on the soccer team*, Wombat thought happily. And as he left the building, Joshua gave him a smile and a quick wave that made Wombat feel like a special friend. *Maybe being different isn't so bad*, Wombat decided as he waited outside. *None of the other boys would have been able to save Hong Lu the way I did.*

When Mr. Lee arrived to take Joshua back to the camp, he was relieved to find Wombat with him. "We were all so worried when we did

not know where you were," he said. "And the boys tried their best to find you. They will be happy to know you have been found."

"I'm sorry," Wombat apologized, for he had not wanted to cause any trouble. But he could not help feeling pleased, too, knowing that the boys had cared enough to look for him.

"Your parents were out when I called them, so they have not yet been told what has happened," Mr. Lee assured him. "When they return my call, I will explain that you are here safe with us."

I wish they didn't have to know that I had been lost, Wombat thought, for he was sure they were going to be very upset to hear he'd been in jail.

"You must be very tired," Mr. Lee said when they arrived at the camp. "You should rest before the soccer practice this evening and get a good sleep tonight before the game tomorrow."

"He doesn't know about the good luck we've got for the game," Joshua whispered, smiling with delight at the secret he and Wombat were sharing.

The good luck we almost had, Wombat thought guiltily. And he decided not to say anything, for he was sure that Joshua wouldn't be his friend once he heard that it was gone.

"It was nice to be liked, even if it was only for a little while," Wombat sighed, after leaving Joshua at the door of his room and continuing down the hall.

"Wombat!" Matt cried out, looking up from the book he was reading as Wombat entered their

room. He jumped up and ran to him. "Where have you been? I've been terribly worried."

"I'm okay. I found Joshua and stayed with him at the animal hospital," Wombat replied.

"At the animal hospital!" Matt exclaimed. "Well, that's too bad. If you'd stayed with us, you would have had a rickshaw ride."

Chapter 11

The next day was the last full day of camp. Even though Mr. and Mrs. Smith would be seeing Wombat the next day, they phoned to make sure he was all right. They were upset to hear he had strayed away from the other boys, but they were relieved to know he was safely back at camp. Before hanging up the phone, they remembered that the soccer match was the next day, and they told him to play the best he could and to have a good time.

How can I have a good time? Wombat thought, knowing the team was going to lose because of him.

Since his soccer uniform was still rumpled and stained with the berry juice from the day before, another extra-large uniform had been found for him to wear, but there wasn't enough time to hem it shorter.

"You could pin it up," Matt suggested, looking at it carefully. "I'll ask Mr. Lee for some pins and I'll meet you on the soccer field."

Most of the boys were already warming up when Wombat got there. The Beijing team had joined the boys from the soccer camp, and as they exercised, they called out to each other, sometimes in Mandarin, and other times in English.

When Matt finally arrived, he brought only the few pins he could find for the uniform. He used two safety pins to hold up each side, then pinned up the hem above Wombat's legs at the front with two straight pins. He used the two remaining straight pins to hold up the back.

"That's the best I can do," Matt said as he looked at where the hem drooped down between the pins. "It would look better if I had more pins. Anyway, be careful they don't poke you."

The teams gathered at the edge of the field, and as the boys on Wombat's team walked past, they touched him on the shoulder.

"That's so they can share your luck," Joshua explained, and Wombat felt more nervous than before, realizing that the boys had heard about the panda.

Wombat had joined the others and took his usual position behind Joshua. After the kick-off, he followed the ball up and down the field, trying his best to keep up with the others. When the first half of the game was almost over, and his team had one goal, Wombat happened to be in a good position to score the second point for his team.

"Wombat!" Joshua called to get his attention and then kicked the ball to him.

Holding his breath, Wombat took aim between the goal posts and swung his foot back as far as it would go. But the sudden jerk to the hem of his uniform pulled one of the straight pins loose, and it jabbed the front of his leg. The sharp pain startled him, and instead of the strong kick he had intended, he only grazed the ball with his toe. It rolled a short distance away, and there was nothing he could do as a boy from the Beijing team reached it. As Wombat stepped

forward to try to block the boy's kick, the pin poked him harder than before.

"Ow," he murmured. "Ow. Ow!" he cried louder as he bent down quickly to remove it. The boy kicked the ball, but instead of it going down the field, it struck Wombat's large rear end. "Ouch!" Wombat squealed as he lost his balance and fell to the ground.

The ball bounced off him, and as it flew to where the Beijing goalkeeper was standing, Wombat was sure he could hear some of the boys laughing. The goalkeeper picked up the ball, and running out of the goal, he threw it a long way down the field to one of his teammates. Because Matt was taken by surprise, the Beijing player had no trouble kicking the ball into the goal to tie the score.

"Don't worry about it," Joshua said as he and Matt walked with Wombat from the field when the first half of the game was over.

"I thought we were supposed to have good luck because of the panda," Matt grumbled, sounding embarrassed because he had not stopped the Beijing team from scoring.

"There isn't any good luck," Wombat finally admitted. "I used it all up, and now there isn't any left for the game."

During the second half of the game, even though he was in position to receive the ball several times, no one would kick it to him. *It's almost like I'm not here*, Wombat thought sadly. *It's because they know I'm a bad player and I haven't any luck to help them.* And he decided right then that if he found good luck in a cookie again, he'd save enough so that the ball would go to the goal instead of the goalkeeper after it hit his rear end. *But*, he thought excitedly as an idea came to him, *maybe I don't need good luck. I've got a strong bottom!*

The game was almost over and the score was still tied when he noticed that Joshua had the ball. Wombat called to him and then ran to stand in front of the Beijing goal, but Joshua hesitated, even though Wombat was in a good position to score a point.

"Joshua," Wombat called again, and finally Joshua kicked the ball to him.

As the ball came toward him, Wombat looked quickly to see where the goalkeeper was standing. Then he bent down the same as he'd done before. As soon as the ball hit him, Wombat swung his rear end around as hard as he could. The ball flew across the field into the unguarded corner of the goal. The game was over. The score was two to one. And Wombat had scored the winning goal!

As he straightened up, Wombat saw all his teammates, followed by the coach, running across the field toward him. He felt very happy when Mr. Chang congratulated him, and the boys all grouped around shouting his name.

They were all very hungry after the game, and the Beijing team joined the other boys in the lunchroom where they were able to get to know each other better. As they continued to talk about the game, they asked where Wombat had learned his special play that scored the goal.

"I didn't learn it," Wombat said proudly. "I thought of it myself. And without any help from a cookie."

✳ ✳ ✳

On the day after the game, Matt looked up from the book on soccer he was reading. "Will your parents be here soon to get you?" he asked as he watched Wombat pack his bag.

Before Wombat had a chance to answer, there was a knock at their door. When he opened it, Wombat found Joshua standing there, waiting to say goodbye.

"I have to go to the animal hospital," Joshua said. "But I was hoping to meet your family."

Wombat glanced over at Matt who had returned to reading his book. "If you did see them, you'd think they're different from me," he whispered.

"My father's different from me too," Joshua remarked casually. "He wants to farm and look after sheep." Then he added quickly, "There's nothing wrong with sheep, but I want to look after all animals – just like I've been doing at the animal hospital."

"If you were an animal doctor, you could work at an animal hospital all the time," Wombat said. "And you could wear a white coat."

Joshua thought for a moment. "Or I could stay home and look after the hurt animals on the

91

farm, and on the other farms too. That would make my father happy, and I'd be happy too."

Matt put down his book. "I wouldn't mind being a sports doctor, but being an animal doctor wouldn't make me happy," he said.

"Being an animal doctor, or a sports doctor, or any kind of doctor wouldn't make me happy," Wombat said. "Not even if I could wear a white coat." He turned hesitantly to Joshua. "That makes us different, doesn't it?" he asked nervously. "Do you mind that I'm different from you?"

"Why would I mind?" Joshua replied in surprise. "Besides, I'm different from you too."

"And I'm different from both of you," Matt said, picking up the soccer ball by his side.

It's true, Wombat thought happily. *We're all different, but we're all still friends.*

"I have to go," Joshua said. "I promised to help with Hong Lu today. She's eating better now, and she's playing too, so she'll be going back to her mother soon." But he stood for a moment without moving. "Goodbye," he mumbled finally as he looked down at the floor. Then he turned quickly, and just as he reached the door, Wombat's parents and Mary stepped into the room.

Wombat was glad that Joshua would have a chance to meet his family, after all. When Mr. and Mrs. Smith had thanked Joshua for looking after Wombat in Tasmania, they walked across the room to greet Matt, leaving Wombat with Joshua in the doorway.

"Maybe I'll write you when I get home," Joshua murmured awkwardly.

"Maybe I'll write you too," Wombat replied.

"Now that you know most of the boys on the soccer team, I can write to you about what they are doing," Joshua added.

"But you don't have any friends where I live," Wombat said. "I won't have anyone to write to you about."

"You can write about you," Joshua replied. "You're the friend I want to hear about."

"And you're the best friend I want to hear about," Wombat said happily.

Wombat could not help feeling sad as Joshua left. But knowing that he would be getting letters from Joshua helped the goodbyes seem not quite as bad.

I wish the other boys could have met my family too, Wombat thought. It didn't matter anymore if any of them thought he was different, he realized as he walked over to where Matt had just finished telling his family about the soccer game.

"I have a friend back home who has trouble kicking the ball too," Matt said to Wombat. "If you visit England, you could show him how you were able to score your goal."

"I'd like to go to England," Wombat replied, glancing at his father.

"Maybe you will someday," Mr. Smith said as he closed Wombat's suitcase.

Wombat picked up his knapsack. "Maybe I really will," he said to Matt. Then he said goodbye and followed his family from the room and to the taxi waiting to take them to the airport.

✳ ✳ ✳

Wombat thought it didn't seem very long before they were in the air and on their way home. After sleeping, and eating, and playing games as before, they finally arrived at the airport, and soon another taxi stopped in front of their house.

It's exciting to be home again, Wombat thought later that night as he lay happily in his bed. But he was sorry to leave China, for he would miss the camp and all the boys. As he thought about Joshua and Matt, he remembered Matt's friend in England who had trouble kicking the ball.

He probably has short arms and legs like me, Wombat thought. *And there are probably lots of others like me too.* He was wishing he could show them all how he had scored the goal, when he remembered the soccer book Matt had been reading. *I could write about my goal in a book*, he thought, *if I knew how to write a book.* And he decided right then that he would learn to write a book, just as soon as he had the time.

Check out Wombat Smith's First Adventure!

Wombat Smith
Vol. 1: Wombat Takes on Tasmania
by Anne Sautel / illust. by Scott Stewart
ISBN: 978-1-897073-32-2

Wombat Smith is the adopted member of a loving human family – but he recently realized he wasn't quite like them. Wondering if he really belongs with the Smiths, Wombat sets out to learn more about what he is – a marsupial. A trip to the library inspires him to travel to the wilds of Tasmania, where Wombat hopes to find other marsupials just like him and maybe a new home. But frightening encounters with unfriendly farmers and Tasmanian devils make the country-side a dangerous place for a lone traveler. Will Wombat ever find out where he belongs?